STOP!

For
Matt and Sarah,
Rosie and Will
with love
J.L.

To   Tamar & Eve,
Astrid & Doogie, Joel,
big Eve, Ben & Simon
Greta & Marco
– who have Not
Read This Book!   D.A.

EGMONT
We bring stories to life

First published in Great Britain in 2009
by Egmont UK Limited
239 Kensington High Street,
London W8 6SA

Text copyright © Jill Lewis 2009
Illustrations copyright © Deborah Allwright 2009
The author and illustrator have asserted their moral rights

A CIP catalogue for this title is available from The British Library

ISBN 978 1 4052 3641 6 (hardback)
ISBN 978 1 4052 3642 3 (paperback)

1 0 9 8 7 6 5 4 3 2

Colour Reproduction by Dot Gradations Ltd, UK
Printed in Singapore

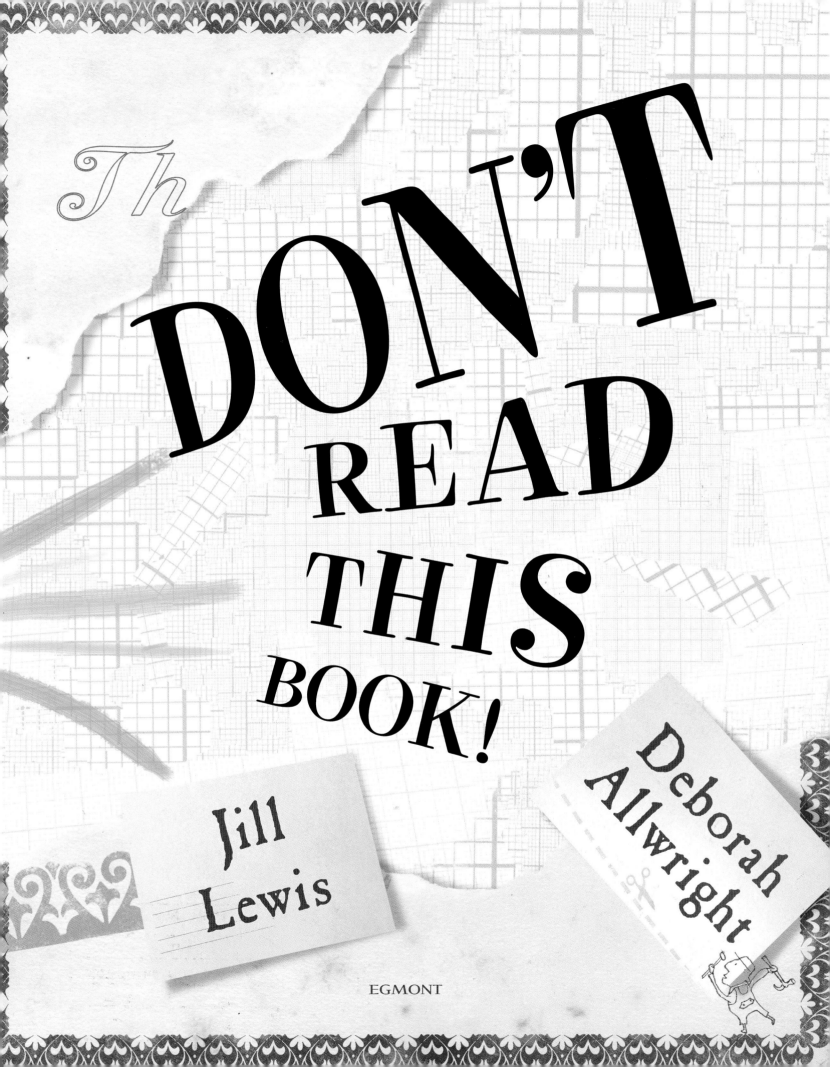

Th

DON'T READ THIS BOOK!

Jill Lewis

Deborah Allwright

EGMONT

Once upon a time

on a dark and stormy night a

STOP RIGHT THERE!

Once upon a time absolutely nothing happened whatsoever! I command you to go and read something else! There is no story here.

But someone had started reading now, hadn't they? (Yes, I do mean YOU.)

The King phoned his story writer.

What do you mean it's not ready? I was promised a new story and a new story I shall have.

The King needed to find his story writer fast because he had the feeling he was being watched . . .

You again!
Go away
or I'll fling you
in prison!

Crumbs - he's cross!

The King met his story writer.

Ah, there you are. My new story is meant to be starting right this minute! Where is it?

Er . . . I had some notes but I've . . . er . . . lost them. I do have the title, Sire. Well, half the title. I had it on this piece of paper here you see, but it's . . . um . . . torn.

The Princess and the . . . Something. What kind of a title is that? Where can we find the rest of it?

The story writer thought hard.

Well, I've just come back from **Beanstalk Crossroads.** I was sitting there thinking. **It might be there.**

What are we **waiting** for?

Let's get on with it.

On the way to Beanstalk Crossroads, the King and the story writer tried desperately to think of the title.

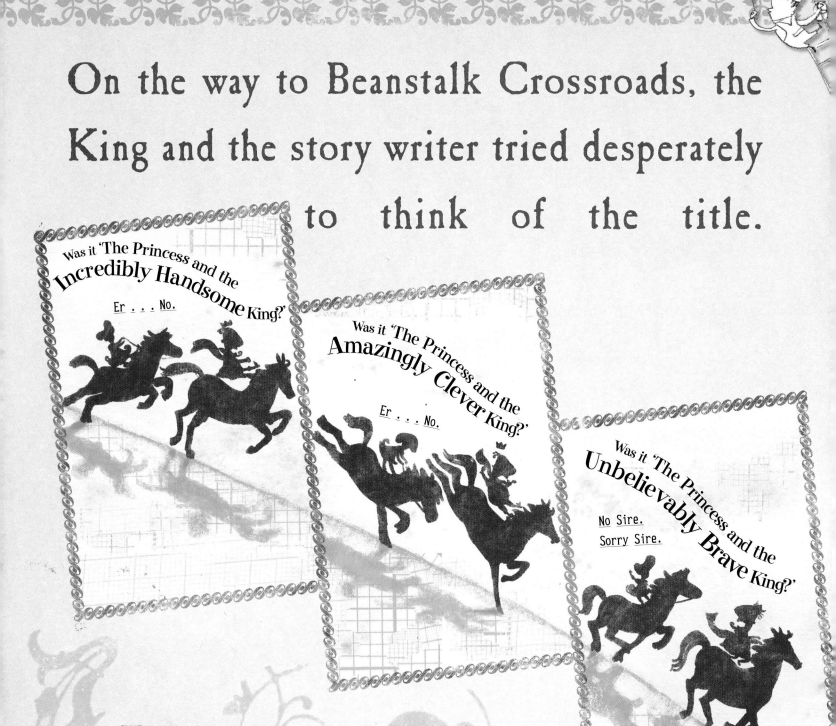

Was it 'The Princess and the Incredibly Handsome King?'

Er . . . No.

Was it 'The Princess and the Amazingly Clever King?'

Er . . . No.

Was it 'The Princess and the Unbelievably Brave King?'

No Sire.
Sorry Sire.

While they were thinking, a certain someone was still reading.

(Yes, I do mean **YOU**.)

Your Majesty, **someone** is watching us.

Don't look.
Keep your eyes fixed to the **front** and keep riding.

page of this book

OW YOU IN
DUNGEON!
Can't you see
there's no
story?
GO
away! No,
wait a
minute!

The writer looked around him.
There were no more pages.
What was he going to do?

IS THIS WHAT YOU'RE LOOKING FOR?

The next two pages! Yippee!
We need . . . let me see . . .
a queen and a prince
and 15 mattresses
and a . . .

FEE FI FO FUM!

We certainly don't need any of that nonsense! Where are we going to find **15** mattresses?

I think <u>Red Riding Hood's Grandmama</u> might have some spare ones.

They raced to Grandmama's cottage . . . . where they thoroughly confused the Wolf.

Er . . . my, my, your Majesty, What fine clothes you have; What smart shoes you have; What a big crown you have . . .

Yes, yes, that's enough of that!

We need some mattresses and we need them now. Get out of bed immediately.

Suddenly the writer came running in.

I've found my notes! We just need one more thing . . .

I thought you were never

coming!

So now we've got everything. We've got all the **characters** and the **beginning** and the **middle** and the **end!** This is so **exciting!**

It's fantastic, it's . . .

Wait

Oh, be quiet. Look! We've run out of space!

We can't tell the story anyway. I am not pleased!

My, what a big **problem** you have.

And we **STILL** don't **EVEN** have the title.

I have an idea.

We can tell it on the last pages.

But we'll have to be really quick.

Oh, and the title.

I've found that too.

It's . . .

The Princes

Once upon a time on a dark and stormy night a princess was struggling through wind and rain to reach the castle of her beloved but because of the storm the King (who incidentally was both handsome and brave) and the Queen of the castle did not believe that such a wet and messy girl could really be a princess.

So the Queen (having taken the advice of her very wise and good-looking husband) decided to set her a test so she asked the royal cook for a pea and slipped it beneath a pile of fifteen mattresses on the bed prepared for the Princess.

because only a princess could have been so delicate.

On hearing the good news the Prince immediately proposed to the Princess,

When the next morning the Princess complained that she'd not slept a wink because of the lump in her bed both the Queen and the King (whose **cunning** and **brilliant** plan had clearly worked) knew she must really be a princess

and the Prince and the Princess were married andtheyalllivedhappilyeverafterTHE **END!**

phew!

WHAT, ARE YOU STILL HERE?

It's your bedtime!

Go away.

And don't you dare read this book again!